ANTONIO'S GENIE

PALMETTO

PUBLISHING

Charleston, SC

www.PalmettoPublishing.com

Hardcover ISBN: 979-8-8229-3702-4
Paperback ISBN: 979-8-8229-3703-1
eBook ISBN: 979-8-8229-3704-8

ANTONIO'S GENIE

TERRANCE A. ROBERTS

TABLE OF CONTENTS

CHAPTER 1

The alarm went off: *Beep. Beep. Beep.* Antonio rolled over and slapped it to the floor. "Fuck, I hate my life," he said.

Today was another meaningless day in his normal life, or so he thought. Antonio was a young adult pothead who worked temp jobs. Today he was starting a new assignment as an inspector of dashboards for a car company. His normal routine was to roll up, smoke, shower, get dressed, and go to work.

Today he decided to take a walk down the road and enjoy nature while he fired up.

Antonio also grew pot, so he decided to also check on his hidden garden. Hiding your garden is very important because you could get robbed. He never grew on his family land just in case someone found his garden and reported it to the police. It was the beginning of spring, and the birds were chirping, and the sun's rays were shining something glorious. Antonio

1

fired up his joint and started to walk down the dirt road with his arms extended, catching all of the sun's rays. As he walked and puffed, inhaling kush smoke, the wonderful herb started to do its part. Antonio took off his knock-off Ray-Bans and stared at the beautiful blue sky. The trees were green again, the air was crisp and refreshing.

"This Bud is pretty good," he thought, cracking a half smile.

Getting to his garden was pretty easy because Antonio planted in the middle of a forest not far from where he lived. When he arrived at his path, he always looked around; he was kind of a paranoid fellow. Going to jail or being fined for manufacturing marijuana is never in someone's plans. Then he darted into the bushes like a scared dog. As he neared his garden, the aroma of a skunk hit his nose. The first time Antonio smelled a skunk, he thought someone was blowing a pound of loud (kush). When he arrived at his garden, he observed his plants to see if any animals were tampering with them. Antonio knew he would have a good harvest this year because his plants smelled great, and they were only two months old.

"You guys are doing very well. You look good and smell great," he said to his garden as he misted them with water. He then fired up a cigarette and inhaled its toxic smoke, then exhaled.

Suddenly he heard leaves rustling. Terrified of snakes, Antonio looked around and spotted a nine-point buck. He bolted without a thought. Running fast and hard, he tripped and fell to the forest floor and slid into a mature pine tree, hitting his head and knocking himself unconscious.

When he woke up the most beautiful woman he had ever seen was standing over him. She had really gorgeous copper-tone skin and hip-length, jet-black hair. She was like a mixture of Halle Berry and Rosario Dawson with the curves of a coke bottle and thick thighs—a goddess to any man.

"How may you serve you, master," she said.

Antonio was lost for words, and his mind was drawing blanks. The first thing he said was, "Am I dreaming, or am I in Heaven?"

"You're very much alive, master. How may I serve you?" She stood there with her arms to her side like a robot. She was wearing a pure white cloudless robe that showcased her perfect-shaped breasts. Antonio just knew this woman was crazy, but he quickly dismissed that thought.

"What does my lady mean?" he said.

"Your wish is my command, master. I will grant you seven wishes," she replied.

Then Antonio stood up slowly, not sure whether he was too high or what. He stood there and stared at the woman, looking her up and down. Then he burst out laughing. She stared back without a blink. "OK, so you're telling me anything I ask you, you can make it happen?" he said, still laughing a little.

"Yes," she replied.

"All right, I want a mill—" He paused. "I want you to be my w-w-w-w—." Antonio paused again. "I'm sorry, what's your name," he asked. "Where did you come from?" He started asking a lot of questions.

"My name is Genie," she replied. "I am from Africa," she also said. Her voice was soft, matching her appearance.

Antonio reached into his pocket and grabbed another pre rolled joint, then fired it up. The first drag he took was long and hard; he inhaled so hard he filled his lungs with kush smoke, then he exhaled. He couldn't believe what was going on. His mind couldn't comprehend what was happening. Surely she was real, but being a genie was unreal.

"OK, come with me, Genie," he said.

"As you wish, master," she replied softly. As they walked down the road, Antonio instructed her to walk ahead of him, and he watched her walk. She was truly a work of art. As they neared his house, he thought about what was going to be his next move. The only thing he had on his mind was *sex*.

Antonio lived with his mother, who was really the only thing he had in his life. Since his brother was killed, he was the only thing she had in the world. She made sure he had all he needed that she could do for him. They didn't have much—just a house his grandparents left her. His father was never around, so Antonio did some things in the street, but he didn't go for a bath. Lucky his mother was out of town at his uncle's house. She never really approved of the women that Antonio messed with; she thought of them as thots. Genie would surely be put in that category as a thot because of the way she was dressed.

When Antonio and Genie reached his house, he directed her to his room. He then asked her to sit on his bed. He had forgotten all about work. Genie didn't have any expression on her face. She just sat there with a blank look, looking around his room. Still not thinking she was a damn genie, he was just going to take advantage of having the finest woman he ever saw in his room on his bed. So he sat next to her and went for the gusto. She accepted his advancements and kissed him back. They started rubbing on each other, breathing hard. He squeezed her breasts. They were very soft. Antonio laid her down and started to suck on her breasts. Her nipples started to harden, and he kissed her stomach and squeezed her breasts some more. When he got down to her vagina, it smelled like honeysuckle. When he licked her, it also tasted like honeysuckle. She moaned out in pleasure, grabbing his dreads. When her body stiffened, he knew she had an orgasm. Antonio's penis was hard as a brick. He didn't think about a condom. He started sucking her bottom lip and rubbing her body, then he pushed himself inside of her.

Genie cried out in pleasure. Antonio moaned in pleasure. He wasn't expecting for her vagina to be that awesome. He pumped and grinded until Genie's body stiffened again. Her sweat even smelled of honeysuckle. He stared at her face, and it was covered with pleasure.

Then he instructed her to get on top of him. She did. She slid her juicy vagina onto his penis, and he grabbed her butt cheeks tightly and sucked her breast. When Genie yelled, "*Yes, master*," Antonio came inside of her.

Antonio didn't go to work that day or even call out, so his job there was no longer available for him. Antonio and Genie made love all night into the morning hours. When he did get up the next day, he was worn out. He didn't even ask anything about her being a genie, but it did seem weird how she'd just popped up in the forest. She smelled so sweet. She wasn't wearing shoes either to be traveling through the forest. There weren't any houses around for at least a couple of miles. Antonio's mother's house sat on five acres of land with a field beside it and the forest around it. It was kind of weird, he thought, for a beautiful woman to be in the forest alone, with no one around for miles. Antonio looked over at Genie. She looked pretty normal—nothing out of the ordinary. He decided to cook them breakfast, so he did. He cooked them bacon and eggs. When he brought her the food, she was already up, standing in the middle of the floor naked.

"Good morning, Genie," he said softly. She replied, "Greetings, master."

Antonio loved when Genie called him "master." It really made him feel like a king—strong and powerful.

He knew he didn't have a job to go back to because it was the first day, and he hadn't even bothered to call in. He felt kind of crazy for even entertaining the thought of Genie being a genie to grant him seven wishes. He thought that it was only three wishes, and if genies were real, why was the world so messed up?

Without a job and with only $444 to his name, he decided to ask her for a wish. He hadn't had much conversation with her since yesterday. It was just sex. Her beauty was unparalleled.

Any men who came across her would want the same; he was sure of that. He watched her devour the breakfast he prepared for her. She still seemed normal, but he was going to play along with the genie thing.

"I wish I had eight pounds of purple kush," he said. Genie stood up and closed her eyes, and just like that, eight bundles of kush were sitting on his unmade bed. In disbelief with his eyes stretched, he slowly walked over to his bed and grabbed a bundle of the sweet violet-colored buds and smelled it. "OMG. This is really happening to me," he said as he looked over at Genie fitness.

"Six wishes to go, master…Are you pleased with this wish?"

Antonio just nodded his head yes. Antonio was very reclusive; he didn't have many friends. After his brother was killed, he almost shut down from the world. He knew a lot of people but didn't trust anyone besides his mother. So what else could he need? He had a beautiful woman literally granting wishes for him.

Money was surely going to be this man's next wish. For centuries every man that summoned her all wanted money and power. He wouldn't be any different, or so she thought. Genie was behind just about every great man in history, and the cycle went as follows: money and power—men craved it. Mansa Musa of Mali was her greatest work. West Africa was where she remembered her existence. Genie could make any man a king and give him what his heart desired. Unlike some of her cousins, Genie loved man and didn't have a dark heart. All the men before Antonio used Genie as a dispensable toy and used her up. Antonio seemed different and seemed to have more feelings. Sure, all of the men before Antonio took her to their beds, but after Money and Power came other women. Genie longed to be set free and to be loved by a man.

Antonio sat with Genie, talking with her for hours about her long, extraordinary life. She was over five thousand years old and told him things that the history books didn't know.

CHAPTER 2

Genie had a personal relationship with people Antonio couldn't imagine.

"So you're telling me 'Voodoo Baby' was all you?" Antonio asked, blowing out a huge cloud of weed smoke.

"Yes," she simply replied.

He told her about his little boring life and how things worked in his time. After he listened to Genie and smoked about half an ounce of his wish kush that smoked like a dream, the sun had gone down.

The whole time they sat and talked, Genie was as naked as the day she was made. Genie is so beautiful and powerful, I don't understand why all those years not one man wanted to have her to himself, Antonio thought. She must be crazy behind all that power and beauty, or the men were just too scared to take control.

Antonio was a romantic. He loved one woman, and when he was younger, he did what youngsters do: mess with a lot of women. When he finally came back to her, she had someone else. Time after time, he would play second fiddle to boyfriends for years. Having Genie by his side, he could go down in history as whatever he wanted to be. Antonio watched Genie through his high eyes and was amazed at himself that they weren't making sweet love all day. She would be his love slave as well as his genie. After that thought he was back on her like a moth to a flame, kissing, rubbing, and groping her until he was inside of her gushing vagina.

Antonio had been with Genie for two whole days. All they did was make love and talk. They barely left his room, much less his house. In those two days, Antonio had fallen in love with Genie for sure. It wasn't because of her unparalleled beauty and the fact that she was going to change his life. It was that out of her power, she was normal. During their time together, he was thinking of a way to take care of her and rid her of the burden of spending thousands of years watching over us.

Being bound to someone with powers like hers and not being able to be free must be hard. So he decided to make three wishes that day. It was time for him to make some more wishes, and the three he was thinking of were pretty good wishes. First he would ask for money, then he would ask for wisdom, and last strength. How much money do you ask a Genie for? he thought. What amount seemed sensible? A couple billion should do it. He wasn't trying to be too greedy. What type of wisdom should he ask for? Does it matter? Just ask to be the smartest person in the world or who ever lived. These wishes were all he needed to take care of and protect her.

Antonio was with Genie for two days, and all he had asked of her was some plants. Genie was starting to feel good about Antonio. He was a great lovemaker, and he just wanted to talk with her and not make wishes. He was a man nonetheless, and he didn't have much, so money was going to definitely come up.

"Genie, I wish to possess the skills to play the guitar better than any man or woman in history," Antonio asked.

"Very well, master. It is done," she replied softly. "You have five wishes left, master," she kindly said.

"Is it done?" Antonio asked impatiently. "Yes," she replied.

Antonio's gait was brisk as he grabbed his guitar. He played a little, but nothing earth shattering. He played a black-and-white Fender Stratocaster just like the ones Leo Fender, Bill Carson, George Fullerton, and Freddie Tavares designed in the '50s. When he began to strum the strings, nothing seemed to be different than the regular skills. Then he closed his eyes and thought of love—his love for Genie—and the most harmonic tune came from his guitar that brought tears to his eyes. When Antonio opened his eyes to observe himself, he watched his fingers move up and down the neck of his old guitar like a spider spinning web. "Wow," he yelled.

"This is amazing," he said with excitement.

With this newly acquired gift, Antonio was sure to impress his mother. Antonio's mother loved music. She also sang in a group back in her day and also recorded a record. She was an extraordinary singer, but she didn't follow it up full time after having his brother and him. Every song that came to his head he played. He did this for hours, playing many of the songs he had ever listened to. Every song he played sounded simple and amazing. This pleased Antonio so much he almost forgot he had a naked genie watching him. He then snapped back to reality when he saw Genie watching him with the realest smile.

God had shined down on Antonio. This type of thing only happened in fictional stories and movies, but as he just watched Genie's warming smile, he knew it was real. Antonio was happy as things were. As of now, money would only complicate his life.

What a kind man Antonio was. His first wish wasn't money, nor was his second. This man might truly be different than all the others. Had she finally come across a man that was sincerely kind and loving? Would he be the one to retire her from her endless job? No, she thought, he was a man. But for now his actions proved different, and it had only been a couple of days. Time would surely reveal this man's true intentions and heart's desires to her.

Today Antonio decided to leave the house with his genie. They were going downtown where the spirit of the city lived. Downtown is also where tourists come to visit a city. Antonio also knew that going downtown, he could show off his new skills and get attention. First things first: let's get Genie into something nice to wear, he thought, but what? He knew he loved a woman who could dress but didn't have the slightest idea what they would wear. Antonio wore a white T-shirt with linen sky-blue shorts, and Genie wore the same outfit. All she had to do was her magic to make any piece of clothing she wanted.

Downtown on a Saturday afternoon was all Antonio needed because everyone was out walking around taking in the sights of the city. The perfect place to get people to listen to him play was the park, and there was where he set up his guitar. As they walked through the crowd of people, it seemed like all eyes were on them, and a lot were. Antonio felt so big with Genie walking by his side. Some people stopped and stared while others just watched. Genie was a real head turner. Antonio wasn't an ugly guy: he was six foot two, with brown skin, locks that hung to the middle of his back, a square jaw, a whole-sleeve tattoo, and intense light brown eyes that he almost always kept covered with shades.

Once Antonio started playing his guitar, people stopped and watched him. He played all types of music that he had learned, and the people loved it. The crowd started to grow the more he played, but when he started to play blues, the people cheered. Everyone was watching, recording him on their cell phones and moving their heads and feet with the melody. He was amazed by the attention. He knew that his skills were good, but the people really loved his music. Before he realized it, he had a crowd of over a hundred people standing around him, and he embraced it with open arms.

Now when he packed up his guitar, some people asked questions, like what group did he play for, how long had he been playing, and does he have music out? As he walked to his car, people pointed at him, whispering like he was from another planet. When he arrived at his 89 Camaro, he packed his small amp and his Fender in the back seat and looked at Genie, and she smiled at him lovingly.

Then suddenly he heard footsteps approaching quickly. He turned toward the steps and saw a skinny young man draped in all black.

"Hold up," the guy said. When he stopped, he put his hands on his knees and kneeled to catch his breath. "Man, that was amazing. You're very gifted, dude. Please tell me you are not committed to a group," he said.

"No, I'm not…why?" Antonio replied.

"Sorry, my name is Martin Lows…I'm a music producer, and I owe a label," he replied as he extended his hand. "My record label is called Lows & Highs Records. I'm local, but I would love to have a sit-down with you, man. Here's my card. Please just have lunch with me, man. I can make you a star…I promise."

On the ride back home, Antonio confided with Genie and got her opinion on what she thought about the offer he just received. Martin was a fast talker, and his mother told him about fast talkers: they all can't be trusted, especially the ones in business. Just that fast, the first day out of the house for the first time playing outside his room, and he had a record deal on the table. Antonio wasn't quite sure whether he was going to take the deal because he didn't know the first thing about the music business.

When he arrived back home, he noticed that his mother was home, and he knew Genie wouldn't be able to stay over with his mother there. He would introduce Genie for show, though the first time he laid eyes on her, he was in love. So he did Love his Mother. She was well spoken, beautiful, well mannered—everything his other friends weren't who had made it that far to even be introduced.

Antonio needed money, but he didn't want to wish it, so he had to come up with some money for him and Genie so they would have a place to stay. His mom's house was out of the question, and he didn't have a lot of friends, so he came up with the plan to sell his weed. Surely that would be more than enough to make some quick cash. He lived in a small town and knew the weed man would love to get his hands on his exotic kush. He could make a killing. His buds were huge and pretty like something out of *High Times* magazine.

Antonio rented a hotel room with the money that he had in his account for a week. So he contracted his weed guy for him to check out his product, and just as he thought, he was happy about it. He smoked a blunt with him and showed him seven grams. His weed guy, Travis Harris, a.k.a. Monster, was a huge guy. He stood six foot seven and weighed three-hundred-plus pounds—nobody you wanted to mess with. Antonio had his pistol (a Desert Eagle) and Genie with him. His Desert Eagle Mark XlX-2 would put down a horse, so Monster would be blown apart—easily—if he got hit with it.

Monster hit the blunt. "Man, this is some good shit, Tonio," he said. "And it looks so official. Really nice; smells great," he said, smiling, knowing he was about to get paid because he'd never smoked anything like it before. Monster stared at Genie like he wanted to take a bite out of her. He asked questions and inquired about how they met and where she was from. He constantly complimented her and angered Antonio, who had a temper.

So they agreed that he would buy two pounds for $5,000. Monster would make that in two days with his plug (contract)—maybe the same day—or sell grams and ounces.

"I will have more of this same shit. Just hit me up, bro," Antonio said, now trying to rush Monster out of his room.

Antonio was not a street dude, but he had a lot of cousins in the streets, and he hung around them and picked up their game. The room that he sold the weed in wasn't where he and Genie stayed. He also chose a rap a around hotel with both sides to it. So you could drive all the way around like a circle, with both entrances open. He sold the weed in the front of the hotel and lived in the back. He never really trusted anyone, but he had known Monster since elementary school. Monster was just as paranoid as he was, and he handled his business very professionally. He had a professional job and sold weed on the side.

"Yeah, you better believe I will, bro. Maybe by next week, I'm gonna run through these packs," Monster replied.

"Imma be knockin' 'em cross the head too 40 a g," Monster said, grinning. "Bet be safe bruh," Antonio replied.

They shook hands, and Monster grabbed his book bag and left the room. Antonio peeked out the blinds to watch

Monster get in his car and pull off. He waited until he couldn't see his car anymore, then he and Genie went to their room.

The next day Antonio and Genie went to the mall to get some clothes. He still didn't have quite enough money to put down a nice down payment on a house that he wanted. In the mall Antonio spent $2,000. Genie loved sundresses and sandals, and he loved Polo gear and Locs (shades). As they were walking back to the car, his phone started to ring.

"Hello," he answered.

On the other end it was his cousin Sleazy, who was a real savage in the streets. He did whatever for some money.

CHAPTER 3

"Man, I didn't know you were raw like dat with the guitar…
and who is dat fine ass bitch all up in yo shit, cuz?" said Sleazy.

"Man, you were in the park? Why you ain't holla at me?"
Antonio said.

Antonio never trusted Sleazy because he was always trying
to run games on people. It didn't matter if he got his name
honestly because he was just that: "Sleazy." He also found
Antonio's brother when he was murdered, and he said he was
going to find answers and never did, and he stayed in the
streets and knew all the killas and dope boys. Sleazy was his
first cousin. They grew up together, and he got some games
from him also, but he was just too smart for his own good.

"Naw, cuz, you on the net, and you got over a hundred
thousand hits since yesterday, fool," he said with excitement.
"Nigga, you hood famous 'n' shit from that guitar shit," he
added, still excited.

"Word," Antonio replied.

"Nigga, yeah," Sleazy said. "Pull up at mama's house and scoop me cuz my phone has been blowing up. Everybody talkin' about it."

"Aight, but I ain't fuckin wit you all day, bruh," said Antonio. "Nigga, pull up," Sleazy said then hung up.

Antonio didn't know why he agreed to go deal with this, but he did anyway. Sleazy was a wild fellow, and he didn't understand why. He had everything he needed: great parents, great upbringing, and he was really smart. He made straight As through school and had a full academic scholarship to college but lost it because he got busted selling loud. When he came home from prison, it was like they'd brainwashed him. He hit the streets running, doing anything for the bread. His mother rewarded him for being smart with shoes, clothes, and cars. It just wasn't enough. He said he fell in love with the streets.

When Antonio pulled up to his auntie's mansion on the hill, Lucius Edward Deeds III (Sleazy) stood at the top of his mom's road talking on his phone. Sleazy's face turned red as Antonio pulled up (he was Mulatto). Then he yelled into the phone and hung up.

"Day he go," yelled Sleazy. "We about to turn the fuck up, cuz." Then he jumped on the hood of Antonio's car, and they rode up to his aunt's driveway. Sleazy noticed Genie in the car but didn't say anything until they got out. "God damn, cuz," Sleazy said as he stared at Genie from head to toe. "Boi, this the girl from the video?" he said, almost drooling.

"Yeah, man," Antonio replied. "You saw the video, and you wanted me over here 'cause what again, bruh?"

Still staring at Genie, Sleazy averted his shady eyes back to Antonio. "How in the hell did you pull her, bruh? You broke, nigga, and this car is a straight bucket, cuz," Sleazy said.

Antonio started to walk toward him with fire in his eyes. They were fighting cousins. Genie noticed Antonio's rage boiling over and touched his shoulder, using her magic, and just like that, he was calm.

"Lu, you called me over to talk shit, or you wanted to hangout or sum'em?" Antonio said. "You know I don't even fuck wit cha like dat anyways, fam," Antonio said. "Cuz you know I gotta fuck wit cha, man, but let's hit the hood. They feeling your guitar shit, Tonio." "Word," Antonio said.

"Cuz, hell yeah," Sleazy said. "Why don't y'all just come chill in the pool house so that I can set everything up?" So they walked through the house to the pool area. Lu did this when he was trying to impress people. None of it was his, but by showing people that he came from well-off parents, he implied that he could also be successful. He could be because he had all the good parts to be successful; he was just too slick.

So after being over at Sleazy's for about two hours listening to him hype things up about their day, they left. The first place they went was "The Wall," which was an old apartment building on the outside of town. It had woods on both sides and behind it. When they pulled up, people were out there drinking, smoking, and shooting dice. Loud music poured out of people's car stereos. Sleazy gave out handshakes and a fake smile, directing Antonio and Genie up some dirty, crumbling stairs. When they reached the top, they entered a room with no doors or windows in it, but there was electricity for lamps. In the room was Sevenfold and his gang.

Sevenfold was the town's biggest drug dealer. He was into everything.

"What's up, Antonio? I'm sure you know who I am… Right?" said Sevenfold. "Yeah, I do!" said Antonio.

"You know I'm making moves out here, getting all this money, huh…" he said.

Sevenfold smiled, showing his diamond slab teeth shining in the lamp's light. Antonio didn't know Sevenfold had a record label. Sevenfold loved music. He had local musicians play at his nightclubs. He wanted to have the first Black guitarist on his label so he could convince him to play with a band. Antonio was his way into Hollywood.

"Imma get straight to it then…I will give you $500,000 to sign with my label with a three-year contract. How does that sound?!" Sevenfold said, smiling.

"*A half M!*" Sleazy shouted. "*Yyooooo*, you serious, Seven?! Yo, Antonio, I already know you are taking that. You rich now, cuz," he said.

"I don't know, man. I got a buddy wanting to make me an offer too," Antonio said. "Who?" said Sevenfold.

"Martin Lows," Antonio said.

"Nigga, I just offered you a half million dollars…you crazy or sum'em?" Sevenfold said.

Then he gestured for his goon to hand him a brownish alligator briefcase. He opened it to stacks of hundred-dollar bills. Antonio already had Genie, and he could use a wish for money. It wasn't about money; it was about playing his guitar. Sure, he would love to make lots of money without a wish. Going through the experience of becoming a rock star with help from his Earth genie but actually playing guitar on stage in front of thousands of people, watched by millions, was unreal—like Genie level.

"You see this bread, bro? *Cash. Yours.* What's up?" Sevenfold said.

"Uhhhh, well, man...fo real. Yo, can I let you know?" Antonio said. Tension filled the room. Antonio looked at Genie. She looked unbothered. Sevenfold's face was stone. Sleazy was about to interject, but Sevenfold stopped him by putting up his finger...his goons were all in go mode. Then suddenly Sevenfold smiled.

"I like this lil nigga, bro...You wanna let me know about giving you a half million dollars *cash*...ahhh ha, ha, ha. But nah, for real tho, I just know it was something special about you, man, playing that guitar, maaann, with your gorgeous girl, man. Good job, by the way, bruh; she's fuckin fine, bruh," Sevenfold said.

Antonio smiled. "Thanks, bruh," he said.

"Yeah...come by my club when you decide or sum'em... aight?" Sevenfold said. "The Chicken Stack is over in Jackson." He then gave Antonio his card. "Do you have a guitar with you now?"

"Naw, it's home, man…sorry," Antonio said.

"Cool…aight, then. Cool, dude. Get with me then…just pull up to the Stack then," Sevenfold said. He and Antonio then shook hands, and Sevenfold and his goons left the room. Antonio didn't want to get mixed up with Sevenfold. He didn't trust him or his cousin. He was going to get in touch with Martin to see what he had to offer too.

On the ride back to his auntie's house, Sleazy couldn't stop talking about why Antonio should take the deal with Sevenfold. He went on and on about the money and how Sevenfold had a record label and how cool a guy he was. Antonio knew a lot came with that money coming from someone like Sevenfold. He'd heard a lot of stories about how he killed people for a lot less.

The next morning, Antonio was woken by his phone. He had smoked and made love to Genie all night. It was noon.

"Hello," he answered with his voice cracking.

"Yes, this is Martin Lows, the white guy from downtown," Martin said, joking. "Yeah, I remember you. What's up?" Antonio said.

"I was wondering if you had time to meet with me today," he said. "Yeah, sure. I was going to call you today anyway," Antonio said. "Cool, dude. Just give me a time and place," Martin said quickly.

"Aight, just meet me at the mall in like an hour and a half…cool," Antonio said. "Sounds great, dude. See you there!" Martin said.

Antonio then got up and showered and got ready. He wanted Martin to know he meant business, so he wore his best garments: an off-white Polo shirt with the brown horse, an adjustable cap with the brown horse, light-brown linen Polo shorts, and brown leather Polo loafers. He didn't tuck the shirt in because he would feel like he was trying too hard. Genie wore an off-white Polo sun dress and leather brown sandals. He had forgotten that Monster was coming by to get some more weed. He could stunt hard now. Monster wanted four pounds, and he was willing to pay $10,000 for it too. He was left with about fourteen or fifteen ounces; that was cool with him. He wasn't worried by Monster buying that much because he had his D-Eagle and Genie.

CHAPTER 4

Antonio's gate was so confident: he had Genie's fine ass beside him and $8,000 in his pocket, and he was on his way to hopefully a million-dollar deal. They met in the food court. Martin didn't look professional at all. He was unshaven, and his outfit was trash. Nothing matched: he had on green slacks with dirty gray New Balance 990s and a navy-blue T-shirt.

"Dude, you have to be the happiest guy in the world," Martin said, shaking Antonio's hand.

"Why do you say that?" Antonio asked, smiling, but knowing the answer. Martin shared that Genie almost made Antonio mad, but he knew Genie was fine as hell.

These guitarists get all the pussy, he thought. The only way she is with him is because he plays guitar. She is too fine. He could tell Antonio wasn't from the streets. Definity middle class—he could tell the way he wore his clothes. He couldn't tell Genie she was from heaven, Martin thought.

"Well, your skills on that guitar are just…I don't know… something. Your girlfriend is beautiful; you dress nicely—very well put together, neat," Martin said.

"Thanks, man," Antonio said.

"OK, let's talk. I just yesterday got a half-million-dollar offer!" Antonio said. "With who?" Martin asked.

"Sevenfold," Antonio said.

"Malcom Strong. You do know he is a drug dealer, right?" Martin said. "I'm pretty sure he kills people too. You shouldn't get mixed up with someone like that to do business with, or anything else for that matter."

"That funny. He didn't tell you he was a killer, but most of your artists never made it big, and he talks about 360 deals," Antonio said. "And to be honest, you look broke."

Martin smiled. "Buddy, I drive an Aston Martin. I live on the west side of Madison!" he said, laughing now. "I tell you what: follow me to my house!"

"Aight, cool," Antonio said.

Martin looked at Genie, then back at Antonio. He pulled Antonio aside and explained to him the number of naked women would be at his Madison that Genie wouldn't approve of.

Antonio looked at Genie, and she smiled at him. He would go, but he wouldn't mess around. He lied to her, made up a story about going to a studio. She agreed to go over to his mother's house to wait for him. Antonio kissed Genie on the lips and stared at her in her hazel eyes. She was just a treasure.

Martin never bought back up the 360 deals. Instead he distracted Antonio with weed and woman, none of whom could hold a candle to Genie. She was just a work of art. Martin did coke right in front of Antonio; the girls did it too. Most of them were skinny white girls, country-ass hoes just partying, looking for Mr. Right, a baller. Martin really did have a Madison, and he drove a gray Aston Martin, but just looking at him, you would think he was broke because of how he dressed; he really did look bummy. They drank and smoked, having a good time. The whole while Martin didn't mention a deal or money, just fun with women, drinks, and weed—Antonio didn't do the coke. Antonio remembered thinking he didn't think this type of shit happened around town. This seemed like some movie shit. It was Monday, damn. He had a great time over at Martin's house.

"You like my car, dude?" Martin asked. "Yeah, it's nice," Antonio said.

"We can go pick one out tomorrow—any color you want. I know I guy," Martin said. "Word!" Antonio said. "That's what's up, though, for real, man."

Antonio was wasted, taking Jose Cuervo gold shots and smoking some pretty good loud; he could hardly keep his eyes open. The next day they went to an Aston Martin dealership. The cars were beautiful, and there it was: all black with a khaki brown leather interior, light tint windows—a 2017 Aston Martin DB11!

"I want this one!" Antonio said, biting his fist. "Done," Martin said.

They did the paperwork. Martin paid with a credit card for it: $214,000.

"If you sign a contract with me, I will have you headlining for Lisa next week. I got the juice, brother," Martin said. "You will make millions, I promise. That car is $214,000. If you sign a contract with me, that's nothing—a toy. You will be working hard, though," he added. "I already got a radio interview for you tomorrow, dude."

He pulled out $10,000 cash and tried to give it to Antonio. Antonio pulled $8,000 out of his Polo heather gray jogger's pocket.

"Naw! I got that already, dude," Antonio said. "Come better than that!"

Aight then, I see now this motherfucker sell a lil sum'em, Martin thought. "OK, this is the most cash I ever even carried on me before," he said out loud. "Sign the paper. I will give you 90K more in your bank account." Martin smiled, knowing Antonio didn't get that money working a nine-to-five.

Antonio smiled. "Two million and you got a deal, bruh!" he said. Martin smiled back. "OK, cool," he said.

Then they shook hands. Damn, he cool with two million, and he just tried to give me 90K, Antonio thought. This guy is shady as fuck, but fuck it: two million is a shit load of money, and I'm on now. I will for sure have to keep my eye on this motherfucker.

The next day he rode through his town in his new car. He drove through downtown with Genie in the passenger seat, cruising. It felt good to have money in the bank and Genie by his side. People stared, but they didn't know who he was yet.

Later that day he had a radio interview to tell the people where he was performing. The local radio station interview was short and quick. Martin had Antonio booked for the next month doing local gigs. One of the first shows was at the downtown club called Havoc. This place had a crowd of punk rockers who loved partying hard. Antonio wasn't anywhere near punk rock, but he was going to rock out every stage he played on. He didn't have any practice with a band; he was a one man show. He didn't have any songs written either. He figured he was going to freestyle it—after all his talent was a wish, but he loved playing.

Martin didn't mind Antonio not playing with a band. It was less he had to pay out, and he knew Antonio was just that good. At the club that night, Antonio was sure to have to crowd in the palm of his hand with the first couple licks.

Backstage Antonio was taking shots of Jose Cuervo Gold because he was nervous. He had smoked like four blunts of kush before even arriving at the club, so he was feeling pretty good. By the time they introduced him to the stage, his eyes were barely open. He didn't have the first idea of what he was going to play. Antonio looked into the crowd, and they stared back; it seemed like an eternity at that moment. And then he started playing. His fingers moved quickly up and down the neck of his Fender Strat—no drums behind him, no bass, just Antonio and his guitar. The crowd loved it. They moved with his every move. It was like they were high and drunk. Martin watched backstage. He looked into the audience. They were under Antonio's spell. He had complete control. It was amazing to see.

"*Wow*, this dude is a rock star, man," the club owner said to Martin.

"Yes, I knew it from the first time I heard him play," Martin said. "Where did you find this kid, man?" the club owner said.

"He's a diamond in the rough—downtown in the park," Martin replied. "He's certainly a gem," said the club owner.

"Yes, he is," replied Martin, looking at Antonio like a bag of money.

Every show that Antonio did, he killed it. His name was starting to spread through his area like a wildfire. Martin worked with Antonio closer than any of his other artists. He spent most of his time with Antonio. Antonio and Genie didn't see much of each other either. He spent almost two years traveling from town to town, club to club, only talking on the phone to his mother and genie. They had money now, and his mother was enjoying her life freely without worrying about money. Genie stayed by his mother's side, and Antonio's mother adored her.

They were the best of friends.

Genie loved spending time with Antonio's mother. She was a very sweet woman.

Antonio had given his mother half of his money. This made her life less stressful, and she had time to do all the things she wanted to do. They shopped for furniture and were always riding somewhere far away. Although she loved being with Antonio's mother, Genie longed to be with him sometimes.

On Martin and Antonio's first day home, they were eating lunch at a local restaurant, and they decided to eat outside. Suddenly two guys walked up; both of them looked angry as they approached Antonio and Martin. Antonio was thinking they may want autographs, but the look on their faces said something else.

"Yes?" Martin asked.

The biggest of the two guys spoke out with a voice of thunder. "Sevenfold would like to speak with you please," he said without any expression on his face. He then gestured to a black truck parked on a curb on the other side of the street. Antonio looked at Martin and looked back at him. What could this guy want but trouble?

Antonio and Martin walked over to the black truck, and they both hopped in. Inside this SUV sat Sevenfold rolling up a blunt but mixing up a white dust substance that Antonio guessed was coke. The truck smelled like loud weed and lingering sex. There were two Asians dressed provocatively. Antonio again couldn't believe this type of thing was happening around his small town.

"You're blowing up, big dogs!" Sevenfold said. "I'm just a small fish, fellows, trying to make it in this music shit. I asked you to fuck with me, Antonio, and was willing to put up a half a ticket coming from this small ass place so you know I'm making moves…And you go to this guy." He pointed his index finger inches in front of Martin's face. "I told you he was dirty. Yeah, I'm telling you in his face—he knows he is dirty. He gon' use you up, bruh, and get paid more than you, and you're the artist. It isn't supposed to work like that.

"Fuck it, though," he added. "I'm good," he said, clearing the bad vibes. Sevenfold lit the blunt and started puffing. The smell was strong.

"Word, that's what up," Antonio said. Martin didn't say much of anything; he just listened. He didn't try to defend himself against what Sevenfold said or anything. The SUV truck was hooked up like a limo inside so everyone was facing each other.

"I could be your security," Sevenfold said. "Or I could let you use a couple of my guys.

I'm the king around here, guys. Like a God or something. I got the juice, guys."

"Aight, cool. Imma call you with details how to get on, aight," Antonio explained to Sevenfold. "We have a lot going on right now, but I tell you what: How about I play at your club, the Chicken Shack, tonight. Sounds good?" Antonio asked.

"That's cool and all, but what about my guys, man? This is a very small favor for a big-time guy like yourself," he said.

"Cool. I will think about it and let you after the show," said Antonio. "Aight, dude. I can respect that," said Sevenfold.

The whole time Sevenfold just wanted to place some spy in Antonio's camp to keep an eye on him—just to keep tabs because he wanted in, and he would get in some way. If that meant getting dirt on Antonio for blackmail, then that's what it would be. I wonder if M give him more money; he ain't got more than me—fucking junkie.

Pulling up to his mother's driveway gave him butterflies. Just knowing his mother was happy made him feel great. She had added another floor and a two-car garage on to the house, paved the driveway to wrap around, and painted the house white with peach trim. It looked really nice. He didn't call because it was a surprise. The big red Chevy truck his mother brought was there, so she was too. His Aston Martin was parked in the garage too. Antonio parked the rental in the driveway and walked up to the door and rang the doorbell. Antonio's mother swung open the door and started jumping for joy; then she started kissing his cheeks. Next came Genie, looking more beautiful than ever wearing a cream sundress with her hair up and tidal big-hoop earrings, no makeup, skin perfectly colored—a goddess. *His* Goddess. Genie jumped right in his arms and kissed Antonio passionately.

CHAPTER 5

Getting ready for the club that night, Antonio noticed that he was becoming a rock star.

He was small but very busy. He needed two phones, for business, Genie, and his mother.

Sevenfold agreed to let him play at his club, and it sold out in hours. He was excited; Antonio could tell every time he spoke with him. Sevenfold asked Antonio about security again but did not get a solid answer.

Looking in the mirror, Antonio stared at himself for a second. He had on four gold and diamond rings: one was a spider, another was the sun custom made on his left hand. On his right and left index and pinky fingers he just had a pyramid 18k gold and the Sphinx 18k gold made with diamond baguettes. The spider body and legs were diamond baguettes set in 18k gold. The sun rays were even diamond baguettes.

His chain was 18k gold beads made of onyx blue and black. He wore $1,000 18k gold custom-made sunglass and $1,500 designer shoes to match his gear. He even started a clothing line: I'm a Jah Apparel.

Antonio walked in his mother's living room, and it was filled with businesspeople, cameras, and people he didn't know. It was unreal.

Antonio pulled up to the Chicken Shack, and it was crazy. It seemed as if the whole city showed up. It took him an hour just to get to the back of the club. People were all in the street filling up the whole block where the club was located. Antonio stepped out of his Aston Martin looking like a million bucks. Genie was on his side wearing a black designer sundress, designer sandals, and 18k gold bangles on her right wrist. He grabbed his guitar from the truck and started to follow his security team into the club.

"Yo, A," someone yelled from the crowd. Antonio turned around, and it was Sleazy, his cousin. He told the team that it was his cousin, and they let him through. Antonio had really blown up in his town; he didn't even thought people fuck with him like that. Sleazy was asking him a million questions, and they went in one ear and out the other. It was crazy how the turnout was. Antonio was still in shock walking to his room in the club. In his room it smelled like weed and sex, just like Sevenfold's truck. Sevenfold had everything set up: a bottle of liquor and a big bag of loud. Genie just stood around watching the scene like she was studying for a test. Antonio had everyone around him, some of whom he knew and who didn't like him. It wasn't a sound check nor a rehearsal, just freestyle music from Antonio.

Now, as Antonio walked out to the stage, he suddenly got nervous. So he stopped and lit another blunt while walking on the stage. The small club was packed, and there were a lot of people in the crowd that he knew from around the small town. Puffing on his blunt, he scanned the audience, then closed his eyes and started fingering his guitar, which he'd named Melody.

The audience went crazy. The noise was so loud it almost drowned out the music. Everything got fuzzy, but he continued to finger Melody till his finger felt raw.

The small building felt like it was about to collapse, but he continued to finger on, driving the vibrations through the air. The vibrations and the roar of the audience gave Antonio a rush that was like sexual intercourse or like doing a cannonball off Mount Everest into the abyss or something, and from then on he was hooked. He would be chasing that feeling from now on.

Antonio was on a plane to LA. Little did he know how his life was going to change. First thing was first: getting a spot to live somewhere nice. Martin had everything set up; all he had to do was choose. He chose this three-bedroom house in the hills with a great view of more hills and houses. When he got settled, Antonio started playing his guitar and smoking weed. By the end of the night, he had set up a small amp on his balcony and played Melody staring into the LA lights as if they were an audience. No one seemed to mind: no one called the police or yelled for him to stop. Before he noticed there were women partying too.

"Do you want some wax," said a skinny but attractive girl. "What's that?" Antonio asked.

"It's weed at its best," she said with a warm smile.

So Antonio took a hit. Damn, I'm getting high as I inhale this shit, he thought. As the weed took its course, Antonio peered into the horizon's lights. Amazing, he thought.

He started choking and coughing up a lung by the second hit. Then, as soon as he stopped coughing he was high as fuck *again* on two hits.

"Wow, that's different," Antonio said slowly. Everyone started laughing at the fact that he was so stoned off one hit. Everything started to get fuzzy, and Antonio rode that feeling for two hours. He was talking with beautiful women, and they were digging him too. These women were so different from anything back home: outgoing and just a breath of fresh air to him. He wasn't famous, but they acted as if he was.

Over the next few weeks, Antonio was attending parties and meeting Martin's music friends. There was no music making, just parties, smoking, and drinking. So Antonio had the idea to get a studio put in his house because it seemed as if he was getting unfocused on music.

The music started after he got into the studio, but all Antonio knew was to play his guitar. He didn't have a singing voice, nor did he know how to put a song together. So he started to get frustrated and started smoking a whole lot of weed in all forms. Before Antonio noticed, six months had passed, and he hadn't really done anything. Antonio questioned Martin about playing at clubs or anything. Martin always told him things were going to change, but they didn't. Then he noticed his money getting low. He was partying so much he didn't think of the money he was spending—and he wasn't making any. That California weed was dam near like his wish weed. It was like a dream to him. The house, weed, and women kept him so entertained he just couldn't stay focused. It was as if he had made it already; there wasn't a dull moment. As long as he had weed and showed off his skills a little, his house was always jumping, or he was at someone else's house.

Then one day Martin called him up and told him to go shopping for something really nice they were going to the Music Awards. Antonio wasn't into wearing suits so didn't wear one. So he wore one of his jogger suits. He was doing well off them back home but not here in LA. The jogger suit was all-white Egyptian cotton, and he had on white leather Chuck Taylors, one gold chain, his spider ring, and his sun ray diamond rings on the index and pinky fingers on his right hand. When they pulled up in a rented Lambo, Antonio started to get nervous, so he smoked a joint filled with moon rock and wax.

Walking up to the event, he started to feel more confident. He saw people from the parties that he attended. The moon rocks also helped out his swagger. He mixed and mingled with everyone he'd gotten to know staying in LA. His circle was very small, and the ladies introduced him to behind-the-scenes guys, which was good and bad because the guys were jealous but talked about him to other behind-the-scenes producers.

Now backstage Antonio rubbed shoulders with some of the hottest artists of his dreams, from R&B artists to rappers. He stood backstage and watched his favorite R&B singer perform and rock the stage. When she was finished, she walked off stage and then they made eye contact and held it for a moment that seemed forever. She was "Liva," a.k.a. Monica Roberts, his crush since high school. She was beautiful and talented. She walked into a crowd of people—makeup artists, designers, and her crew—that surrounded her, talking to her about her next move.

What was that stare she gave him? Antonio thought maybe it was the weed or maybe not, but he wanted to know. She had been dating her longtime boyfriend of many years for almost her whole career. He was beside himself and cheated on her, and she never did date again, just made back-to-back hits. I guess that's what makes a good artist and music with real feeling in it. All the songs he heard had so much hurt in them, and Antonio loved sad songs. They just invoke feelings he loved—good or bad, just deep feelings. Some of her songs dogged men, and those songs were the ones that made her name and stayed on the charts the longest. I guess she was thinking, If it wasn't broke, don't fix it.

Genie longed to be with Antonio. Even though he called every day, he hadn't been home since he left. Out with Antonio's mother in the mall, they ran into Sevenfold and his goons.

"Hello, ladies," said Sevenfold.

"Hey," said both Genie and Antonio's mother.

"I see you ladies are here shopping. What the move for tonight?" he asked. "Church," Antonio's mother said.

Genie knew Sevenfold's type all too well. He loved power more than anything. He surrounded himself with big bad guys that he controlled with his fingers and eyes. He was surely a bad guy, a killer, a war starter and finisher. She stared him down from head to toe in disguise—at least she thought she was because she noticed he stared right into her being.

"Well, I wanna come too," Sevenfold said.

"Huh…you don't seem like the church type, young man, but who am I to judge?" Antonio's mother said.

"I'm sorry. My name is Malcom Strong," Sevenfold said, extending his hand. "There's a first time for everything, ma'am."

"Ohhh, first time!" Antonio's mother said.

"Yes," Sevenfold said with a smile showing his diamond teeth. "Well, in that case service starts at seven tonight," she said.

"All right I will be there at seven," he said, giving Genie a stare down before walking away.

"I hate to judge, but that young man may be a drug dealer," Antonio's mother said. Genie said nothing; they just continued shopping. What was she thinking even giving him that small window? He would surely try to make a move. Antonio was sure to meet someone on the road living his new life. She quickly dismissed that thinking: he was in love with her. She could tell the way he looked at her and touched her. Of all the kings she'd made, she could truthfully say that he was the one for her.

Walking through the north side of town thinking to himself, he had to still be selling weed and robbing people and his cousin in California. Sleazy was really starting to feel some type of way. He put all that work in to get Sevenfold to talk with this nigga. Now he wants to act brand new with Martin, driving around town in his Aston Martin. All the times he smoked weed with him and put him on bitches, and this is the thanks he gets. His mother bought him school clothes, paid his mamma's mortgage, helped her get cars, and helped pay for them. They washed together and stared at the same bed whenever his parents went out of town or just for the weekend, even summer breaks from school. They were like brothers. Now Antonio wants to turn his back on me because he is getting a little famous, Sleazy thought. I watched his back like his brother did—probably more, cause his brother was six years older than him.

His phone started to ring. "What up, fool? You ready to hit these niggas up?" the voice said.

"You already know," said Sleazy. "These niggas think they can come around here, set up shop, and don't fuck with us. Hell naw, they about to feel it today, bo! I'm on my way over Tina's house now to go over the plans," he added.

"Aight," the voice said.

What Sleazy didn't know was that the guys they planned to rob were in town dealing with Sevenfold, and they stayed out of the way because he was doing a favor for a team of African guys he owed money to. It was also a power move because if people knew he owed money, it would make him look bad. In this type of work, the first sign of weakness was like blood in the water filled with starving sharks.

Around Tina's now, Sleazy began to go over the plan with her and her "Rat Pack." Tina was a caramel-colored big-boo-ty tattooed striper from Florida he fucked with. She was all about the money. She had been setting guys up for years with Sleazy. It was her side gig.

The plan was to meet these guys at the club and have a flock of girls flirt with the guys, but Tina would be the only girl to actually go through with flirting. She would have friends to entertain her friends. Then they would kidnap the mark and hit his money house.

At the club that night, The Shack, Sleazy sat at the bar and watched Tina and her girls in action. They were doing good as they normally did at home clubs; they were more comfortable and aggressive with the guys. Sleazy had a thousand scams. Sevenfold wasn't in on this because it was his club, and he would want some of the cut or would be pissed because it could also make him look bad.

This one guy Sleazy noticed always kind of glanced over at him, but he paid it no mind. He was with the set of marks—at least he thought he was. Sleazy left and went around back to slip into a hidden room Sevenfold made to watch the club. By the end of the night, Sleazy's Rat Pack had the guys gripped and ready for the plucking.

The guys took them to the nicest hotel in town. Sleazy got a text that the guys had guns and they were really bad asses.

He texted back, "Bitch, get ur shit together and close this shit…hmu when to kick the door in."

CHAPTER 6

Tina texted back, "K, bae," followed by water and kitty cat emojis.

Knock, knock, knock…

"What the fuck?" someone said.

Someone peeked through the peephole. There stood the guy from the phone earlier that day.

"Who the fuck ordered room service?" the voice said. "I did," said Tina's voice.

The locks started to unlock, and the door flew open. There stood one of the marks with a chrome .357 pointed at the guy's head with the hammer pulled back.

"Yeah mufuca ain't shit sweet here, bitch," he said smiling, showing off a mouth full of diamonds and gold. Gimme this shit, he said as he reached for the cart. He couldn't see outside the room until he reached for the cart. On the side of the door was Sleazy and his pack of wolves waiting like hungry wild dogs.

Crack. Sleazy smacked the mark with the bottom of his gun from the side of the door, splitting his forehead. Then sleazy grabbed his other gun from his hip, and as the guy fell back,

Sleazy's team rushed in. The room went off like the Fourth of July. First hit by Sleazy's team was the door guy. Sleazy jumped behind a couch. Damn, it wasn't supposed to happen like this. It was supposed to be a stickup, and they were supposed to give it up, but they started busting.

Back in LA, Antonio was in his studio, smoking weed and playing guitar. He had now hired a drummer, keyboard player, and bass player. He had a whole band now. The keyboard player was his longtime friend from back home. Now Antonio was just playing shed sessions in his studio. Then his phone rang.

"Hello," Antonio said.

"Are you sitting down?" said Martin on the other end.

"Yeah! Why?" Antonio said.

"Where are you at?" Martin said.

"In my studio, Martin! What's up, bro?" Antonio said.

"Liva's people got in touch with me and told me she wants to have a meeting," said Martin.

"Yeah, right," Antonio said. "A meeting with Liva."

"Yeah, man, I swear on my dick, dude," Martin said. "But get your shit right, pal. Smoke that weed till it makes your fingers do what they do," he added, joking. "But for real: a meeting at the studio tonight at ten."

"*What studio?! My studio?! Martin, for real? Tonight? Damn*," Antonio said.

"You got this shit, kid. You're the best guitarist I ever heard or saw in my life. Didn't I tell you that something was coming? Not this big, but I just knew your talent alone was something out of this world, kid," Martin said, getting choked up. "I will be over there in a couple hours," he added, then hung up.

Antonio just sat there holding his phone, processing his phone conversion with Martin just then. It was really her, and she was coming to his house.

Antonio knew he had to be fly when she came by. Then he thought about his skills on the guitar because of Genie, and she was back at home waiting on him, and she was a genie. That's what he had to tell himself at the award show—a crazy cool fun night, one of those never-forget nights, even though you're high as fuck.

Later that night Antonio had smoked about half an ounce of that California rapper weed, and he was ready for whatever was going to happen that night. He had on his best outfit, one of his jogger suits: black with yellow around the collar, wrists, and ankles. He wore black leather Polo shoes that looked like Chuck Taylors. The logo on his jogger suit was of a black man holding a guitar under the sun, and the sun cast a shadow of the man with wings. He wore all of his rings and one gold rope necklace. When Liva and her people pulled up to his driveway, things got real really fast. She brought three more women with her and three bodyguards. The paparazzi were everywhere, and they came from nowhere.

Inside the studio Liva began to talk about wanting to meet with Antonio. She basically wanted to record three songs using just the band, no machines for music. She wanted something soulful and vocal, kind of old school. She introduced herself as Monica Roberts, and the three women with her were longtime friends.

"To be as country as you are…you don't seem intimidated by me at all," Monica said. "It's Cali, bud," Antonio quipped with a smile.

"Well, why are you holding back? Blaze up then!" Monica said.

"Oh, aight…I didn't know," said Antonio.

"Wow! What planet are you from, bro? Hell, yeah," she said.

She was really down to earth for a mega star. She also wore a heather gray jogger by PINK.

"I have a confession," Monica said. "I had you looked up after I saw you at the awards show. I'm so sorry; it's just that…"

"You really don't have to explain. I figured as much. I'm a guitarist from the sticks of nowhere," Antonio explained, licking the joint together.

"Wow…smart, talented, and handsome—you're a triple threat to these guys," Monica said.

She was really flirting with him at this point. They locked eyes again…then Antonio lit the joint. Monica wasn't Genie but was close. She had dark skin, like dark chocolate—beautiful

47

skin—and a great smile. She was smaller than Genie but built just right. She was like Jessica Alba, Megan Fox, Meagan Good, and Bernice Burgo: Good's lips, Burgo's body (slim thick) and skin, and Fox's face. She was very stunning.

Now on their third joint, Monica asked Antonio to play something on the guitar. This made Antonio nervous, but then he thought she was just really cool and laid back. And that's what he started to play: cool, laid-back vibes. Monica started to hum and sing a little.

Monica thought, Wow, this guy is fine as hell, talented as hell, and smart. I know he has women and children everywhere. A smooth guitarist from the country in LA—he must be doing OK. There were two 2017 Aston Martins parked in the garage, not the driveway. This is his studio and his house in a nice neighborhood. He's a winner. He's doing well for himself.

Hollywood would crew him up, though. He was just a little wet behind the ears, but a nice guy with great vibes.

Martin was in the background watching them socialize. He entertained the women and the guys he had in his shed sessions. This young man was truly amazing, Martin thought as he watched Antonio play for Liva, the hottest pop star of this time. He watched her enjoy Antonio playing with this band he suddenly had. She was actually laughing and flirting with Antonio. He took it very well too. He was like a god hidden in that little town waiting to be found, and Martin did—he found a star.

This was going to be huge: making a *couple* of songs—wow! After they made these songs, everyone would be able to hear and see Antonio's talent. Every artist would want a song with them. And he was charging top dollar too. This is really happening, Martin thought. He almost couldn't keep it together, the more he kept thinking of the possibilities these moments held. Monica was very cool too. Her bodyguards were like her friends. They actually talked with everyone. She was really into Antonio, though, laughing at everything he said and touching him; it was so cool to watch.

On the run now, Sleazy had to get Sevenfold involved. They had killed Tina, and two of his boys were shot and in jail. He had to leave town because one of his boys wasn't going to handle the time. Antonio would have to come through for him now; he needed him. He couldn't believe Tina died. He really loved her. She was very smart and down for him to the fullest, and she died for him. He only had about $17,000 in cash, enough to get him started somewhere in California. Turns out the mark was bigger than he thought: he was working for the African cartel and had been running two money houses in the small town. They were all dead except for the main guy.

Sevenfold was connected, but nothing like these guys. But he had to pay for killing Tina—on his life he did, and before he left town, he would have to settle that score.

Sevenfold was livid that Sleazy had fucked up. He was going to find him and serve him to his debtors. They were going to come and burn his little town up. These guys were really from hell and would stop at nothing to get what they wanted. He was really livid because he had no idea Sleazy did the whole setup at his club. Or was this a play to get him out of the way so he could be the big man? Sleazy was a very ambitious young fellow but just too smart till he was dumb. Then it dawned on Sevenfold that he was behind all of the deals falling apart. He was still around somewhere close. He was pissed about Tina getting killed and not thinking right. That would be his downfall: getting his emotions involved.

Martin had snorted an eight ball of coke and was wired, thinking, now how was he to tell Antonio about him and Sevenfold? Sevenfold was his old running buddy from back in the day. They used to sell dope together, fuck girls together—really everything. Sevenfold wanted to be a kingpin, and he just wanted the money. Sevenfold wanted power and respect too. Martin just wanted money—enough money to not work anymore. See, Martin's father was a plumber and died with nothing had he not stepped up to be the man of the house. His mother was pretty and settled his father from being a street thug. He got a job after getting shot by one of the other street thugs in the neighborhood. That was the night Martin met Sevenfold in the hospital: his mother had been stabbed and raped.

CHAPTER 7

Martin was outside in the back of the building smoking a cigarette and saw Sevenfold crying. He was sitting on the side-walk after a summer rain, crying his eyes out, sobbing with such pain in his cry. He sobbed so badly until he fell over in a puddle of water. He was so weak he could barely sit up, and the pain was so deep. He had walked in on a trick stabbing his mother. He would never forget the look in the trick's eyes as he walked over to him with his five-inch knife dripping with his mother's blood. At that moment he felt so helpless and afraid.

"Hey, man, what's wrong?" the kid Martin asked the kid Sevenfold.

"I hope my mother doesn't die. Social services will take me and my baby sister and split us apart," the kid Sevenfold said.

"You want a cigarette?" the kid Martin asked.

"Nah, I heard those things will kill you and rot your teeth," the kid Sevenfold answered. "I got this blunt that you can smoke if you wanna smoke something."

"I never smoked weed before," said the kid Martin. "What will it make me feel like?" "Good," said the kid Sevenfold. "Like you're asleep but not asleep; like you're dreaming in real life," he explained.

"OK," agreed the kid Martin.

From that night on, they were like two peas in a pod. If you saw Sevenfold, you saw Martin. Sevenfold also had to fight because the kids picked on him for hanging with a white kid. Martin had seen him cry and at his lowest and never picked on him or even bought it back up.

See, Sevenfold's mother was a whore and a heroin addict; he had to grow up fast to take care of his sister. She grew up and also started doing drugs and overdosed. Sevenfold felt it was his fault because he was too busy trying to make money to spend time with her, and he sold the same drug she died from: heroin.

Sleazy was still around his area but kept away from his hometown. He had found out that Sevenfold was looking for him. He was making himself hot for interfering with Sevenfold's deals and could give up his location, and that would be the end of him. He didn't have any allies; his closest hitters were in jail or dead. The few that could help out would sell him out because they didn't have loyalty, and for a few bucks, they'd kill their grandparents, so he stayed away.

They weren't as smart as he needed them to be either but were ruthless. He knew Sevenfold would stop at nothing until he was found. The greatest advantage he had on him was he was smarter. He used drug addicts to set up his businesses, so there was no way Sevenfold could find him: the junkies were so drugged up they couldn't remember his face or the day before for that matter.

Waking up, Antonio looked over and stared at Genie. She was so beautiful. He was always so amazed that Genie was so overwhelmingly fine. What was he going to do today? Maybe take a ride to a distant town somewhere out of town. Antonio was also thinking about how he could stay away from her for so long. He then sat up and showered. When he got out of the shower, Genie was awake and sitting up in bed waiting for him. He walked up to her, drying himself off.

"Genie, have you used magic on me…ever?" he said.

"No, master," she said quickly. "Why would you ask me that, master?" she asked, sounding kind of hurt.

"Oh, it was something I thought about before I decided to come home," he said.

Antonio never could really figure out if she was or wasn't, and because he kissed Monica, would she know? Or did she already know? He didn't know if he liked Monica or if it was because she was "Liva" the world's most talented singer of his time. Antonio could tell Monica kind of liked him, and it was amazing that that was possible. He had a little buzz home and back West. He was not really a rock star, but he kind of felt like one.

"Well, if you were, what would it be, you think?" he asked.

"Nothing, master. I don't have a reason to use magic unless you asked for a wish," she kindly said.

"OK, but you never get tired of just being here with my mother all this time?" he said with a little conviction.

"Your happiness is all I want, master. You would take me with you if you wanted me to be there with you. You didn't, so there's no reason for me to ask you, so I don't bother," she said. "I know you love me. I can tell the way you talk to me, the way you touch me.

"To be honest you are the only man in many, many centuries to take this long to make wishes. You only made two wishes in three years' time, and they were very trivial things. Does that make sense to you, Antonio?" Genie asked.

"Antonio," he said. "You never called me that before."

The next thing Martin realized, he was waking up off the floor, and he was bleeding from his nose. He looked in the mirror, and he was still a little fucked up. He walked in the hall of his apartment and tripped over a naked woman in his hallway. When he got his composure, he noticed that his living room was full of women; he counted five. He couldn't remember what happened the night before, but he was still jacked up on coke and he counted about seven women in his apartment and not one sign of a condom. Martin staggered back to his bathroom to his medicine cabinet, grabbed his bottle of Lortab 10s and popped three of them. Next he rolled up a blunt with a Lortab crushed up in it. As he smoked his laced blunt, he thought about himself and Sevenfold in the old days. The memories started to fade back in like a crashing wave.

"Man, I think me and you can rob a bank," Sevenfold said.

"We got the guns," he said.

"Yeah, right; we are good at selling these Os," Martin said.

"Naw, man, for real we can do it," Sevenfold said. "All we need is an alibi."

"I know this bitch that will do it. She down; all we gotta do is break her off a lil some'em, and we good. She has been working there nine years, man. She knows how the whole thing operates," he said.

"It just seems like a lot because it's a bank in an old county town. We can do it bro!" "Just think about it," Sevenfold explained. "750,000K. Easy bro!"

"Man, that's a whole bank though," Martin explained. "With only two people...sounds crazy, bro. Ain't no way that's gone happen dude," he said, dismissing the thought. "Sound Strech as fuck, bro."

"350,000K checkmate M," Sevenfold said.

So there he was, about to rob a bank in Glide County, a little town 451 miles south of their hometown. They had fixed up an old '96 Honda Accord; they spent five thousand to upgrade the motor. They drove the car in a trailer. They unloaded twelve hours before the robbery, then drove up closer to town. Martin was armed with an FN57 and jacked up on cocaine. Sevenfold was armed with an AK47 with a seventy-five-round drum. Sevenfold was focused, hyped, and ready to make his debut. He would kill someone to make his caper successful.

Sevenfold ran into the bank and fired three shots into the ceiling. There were a total of eight people in the bank. Martin ran and grabbed the president of the bank and rushed him straight to the safe-deposit room. Sevenfold had gathered everyone in the middle of the bank. In one minute Martin was in the vault to get the money. Right before they left the bank, Sevenfold fired twelve shots in the ceiling to let them know he meant business then ran off. They were in the car in three minutes and fifty seconds. They were dressed as ninjas to be cocky. In the car now, they were burning rubber toward their trailer, which was waiting. The sheriff or law enforcement in the small town couldn't respond to the well-crafted caper. Off that robbery Sevenfold and Martin profited $800,000 cash money. They flooded the streets with cocaine.

Sleazy was living with a pretty little accountant five counties away from Sevenfold then, he remembered. Sevenfold had a junkyard, and he kelt 100,000 thousand. If he knew he was around, he probably moved it, but if he knew he was in town, he would've been dead Sleazy. So he decided that he would go for the money. Sevenfold probably was so busy looking for more ways to get paid. Sleazy knew Sevenfold was a cold killer with intense force. Sleazy looked up to Sevenfold because he was a go-getter, just making shit happen, getting shit close. On to the next thing: that's how Sevenfold had so much power because he would come at problems with overwhelming force. So Sleazy made the move. He went in the daytime looking around the junkyard with the other customers, looking under the hoods. He had a toolbox and everything really into charter, and he wore a hoodie. Sevenfold had added cameras everywhere. Sleazy couldn't make it happen that day; he had to try something else. After hours was going to have to be the next move.

Antonio had learned what happened with Sleazy and Tina and some of his boys. He also learned Sevenfold wanted to go after Sleazy because he was hot. Drawing attention to them made the town hot, losing business. What was he to do? He couldn't let his cousin get killed, and he didn't want death, and he didn't want any voice or shooting.

So he got a meeting with Sevenfold. Antonio took Genie with him as well. His plan was to let Sevenfold be head of security; that would probably persuade him to at least calm down, to buy him some time. Antonio didn't speak with Martin about his choice on the matter.

They met at Sevenfold's club, the Chicken Shack.

"So you heard about Sleazy, huh?" Sevenfold said. "That motherfucker just gave birth to a rotten man. He let his wit get the best of him. He's caused a lot of trouble between me and my plug, and that can't happen, you feel me?" Sevenfold said calmly.

"How about I make you head of security?" Antonio said.

"Well that's cool, bro, but I need your cousin's head, sir," Sevenfold said with a sinister smile, his diamonds dancing in the light. "I just gotta have him," he said once more.

Tension built in the room.

"I know you haven't heard from him because he knew I had this covered," Sevenfold said. "I got a feeling he's not too far away because some of my spots have been getting robbed, but I can't get to him. It's some people out here really want to just smoke 'im. I want him alive, but others don't. He thinks he's so wise he will stay right under your nose," Sevenfold explained as he walked closer to Antonio and Genie.

"He killed some very important people in that room, man. These people will stop at nothing to get him. People you love will die in the name of Sleazy, man!" Sevenfold said. "He's dead already," he added.

At that moment, Antonio would have to figure out whether he should make another wish: money.

"Listen, how much you think they would take in cash for this issue?" Antonio said. "Man, you don't have enough money to pay these people," Sevenfold said, smirking.

"Try me," Antonio quipped.

Genie could tell Sevenfold meant business; this man was very strong willed. He showed mercy because he wanted something out of the deal. She knew Antonio's big heart was going to make a wish for his cousin's life. Sevenfold was going to squeeze a dollar out of the deal as well. Genie wasn't going to tell Antonio what to do; she was hoping he would know. If he asked for the wish, she would grant it.

"Let me make a call then," Sevenfold said. "To be honest, the motherfucker doesn't even deserve it. His name speaks for itself," he quipped.

Antonio looked over at Genie. She was wearing an off-white romper with off-white "I'm a Jah" slides; the romper showcased her thick thighs. Her rumper was also an "I'm a

Jah" brand. Antonio held up three fingers to Genie; she just said yes. He was going to make his third wish on this guy.

Sleazy sat in the living room of his girlfriend's house. "This motherfucker ain't found me yet! Imma kill his ass quick. I bet he did come to Antonio too since he came home. I think Imma kill this motherfucker tonight; that shit he gotta go!" Sleazy thought aloud. He walked to the bedroom to his dresser drawer and opened it. Three Polo drawers and socks were in it at first glance, but there were guns and money as well. Sleazy grabbed his twin 1911s. They were blue steel with the letter L carved in the oak handle. He then choked back each one, putting a bullet in each chamber. He holstered the big pistols then walked back in the kitchen and poured a glass of Seagram dry gin and orange juice. Then he walked to his coat rack and put on a black zip-up jacket. Sleazy walked outside of his girlfriend's house, locked the door, then turned around. *Pop, pop, pop.* Sleazy was thrown into the front door from the impact of the 9 mm bullets hitting him in three different places.

Martin had to tell Antonio his past with Sevenfold. To be honest he was surprised Sevenfold didn't tell him. They fell out over money and a woman of course. Sevenfold had stolen $500,000 from him and had been fucking his girlfriend. He in turn shot Sevenfold in the chest; the bullet missed his heart by inches. He walked up to Sevenfold on Old Progressive Road and shot him down in the street. He then ran away and left town and got hooked on cocaine and pills. Martin needed to come clean because they were about to make some serious money-making songs with Monica. The song itself would take off, and he and Antonio needed to be on a good level of trust, Martin thought.

"Ooh yeah, baby, suck that dick," Martin said, driving down the freeway in his Aston Martin.

He was also beginning to love LA—the women, the weather, and the fame and clout he was about to get as well. Antonio couldn't have come to Martin at a better time. He was about to skip town anyway because it was too much of a reminder of his old self. Sure, he still partied and get fucked up, but he wasn't like a shadow of Sevenfold—some street thug. Martin wanted only the money, and fame from Antonio's success would be the icing on the cake.

It was good to know that he would have to kill people to get what he wanted or have any worries about money. Sevenfold was out there still trying to be the biggest drug dealer; he hadn't grown up and set higher goals.

That day when he and Antonio were in the back of Sevenfold's SUV, he thought he was a goner. Now that was a shocker. He must've realized his wrongs from the .32 to the chest—nothing like near death to help you realize comma is real.

Sevenfold walked back into the room smoking on a Perfecto cigar and holding a glass of cognac.

"Well, my people did come up with a number, and they are giving you a week to come up with the money, but they want $30 million," Sevenfold said.

"Done," Antonio said. "I can have it in three business days sir. And this is it with my family," he also said.

"Sure," Sevenfold said quickly. Then he realized Martin was Antonio's manager. "Damn, man, Martin got it like that. He always knew how to get some money now, but *fuck*!" Sevenfold said. "That motherfucker sitting on nothing less than $50 million. I gotta get a part of that shit, music shit. Ain't no way he's been making that much from this kid. He got to be still dealing with some major plugs."

"What you mean by 'he always knew how to make money'?" Antonio asked. "Why don't you ask him, dude?" Sevenfold said. "Y'all done made all this money together, and you still don't know who you are working with?"

Sevenfold still wanted Sleazy's head and money but not $30 million, just $10 million. I wanna fuck his bitch too; that hoe the finest thing I done seen in real life, Sevenfold thought. He would've fed him and that bitch to those Africans they played in games. Maybe Martin could give him his plug; he could at least do that.

"OK, Imma be sure to do that too," said Antonio.

Monica couldn't believe that she had let a little country ass boy steal a kiss then liked it. What was wrong with her? Your Monica is the best thing since wonder bread! How? I mean really! How? But he was so fine and talented—so, so talented. He actually makes you seem like you can play that guitar. He's a nice guy; he definitely takes me in well. I got to see what this country lil bitch got over him. Fuck that—I want him, and I will have him, Monica thought as she sat in a meeting about some business of her friend's; she asked her to attend because it was her. What kind of man could stop himself in the middle of a kiss with the biggest pop star in the world. He will have to explain himself for it, but a phone call wouldn't do it nor a text message. So she decided at that moment on the PJ to vacation to Paris with some of her billionaire friends.

CHAPTER 8

Why did 'L' have to get into this much shit? Thanks to Genie, his ass was saved, thought Antonio. Now he had to make another wish. Fuck it—Antonio had the power to help, so he did. Now people would think he was rich. Antonio also thought he would have to move his mother and Genie to California so he could be closer to them. Sleazy would have to be far away from him. To think about it, he didn't even get in touch, not even a text. He was going to have the whole county thinking he was a rich superstar. Antonio pulled up to the drop off with Genie in his mother truck. The money was in all hundreds: thirty bags of one hundred $10,000 stacks.

Antonio just drove with the duffel bags in the cab of the truck. The truck came with a hard-top cover. Antonio knew his mother loved to do different little things in the yard, etc. Sevenfold had him arrive at the warehouse he owned. He used it to hold goods for different places. It was storage for a freight trucking company. Genie was stunning as usual. She wore dark denim jeans ("I'm a Jah" brand), a black halter top with the words "Cream of the Universe" ("Im a Jah" brand) in white letters, and high-top black-and-white Vans. Her skin glowed in the warehouse lights. Antonio was still holding his D-Eagle pistol, but he had Genie also; he knew she would use some magic to save them.

"Damn, this dude brought his old lady," Sevenfold said jokingly. "That's some gangster shit. Your little ride-or-die chick," he quipped.

Sevenfold was four deep. They all stood on each side of Sevenfold's SUV. Antonio was a little nervous. This was tense— far from anything he'd ever had to do. Genie was standing beside him looking on bothered; that eased Antonio's nerve.

"Yeah this my baby, my world here, man," Antonio said. He was just trying to make the process move along; he needed it.

Two of Sevenfold's guys checked the bags.

Sevenfold tried to make small talk. "So you and Martin are doing really well," Sevenfold said. "Thirty million in three days, with a one-day notice. Man, that's pretty fuck out of this world. I mean to be honest, I believe you are selling major weight with him."

"Man, Imma also be honest: I don't give a fuck," Antonio said. "Just give me my cousin so we can get on with life."

Then Antonio's phone rang. It was his mother's ringtone. "I have to take this call; it's my mother," Antonio said. "She probably could tell something wasn't right when she left the house. Imma just let her know I'm OK."

"Hurry up, little motherfucker. I gotta get these people their money," Sevenfold said. "Tonio," his mother said. Antonio could tell when she spoke his name something was wrong.

"Yes, Ma," he asked.

"It's Lucius: he was found shot up in front of his house," she said crying now. "OK, Ma, Imma call you back," he said then hung up.

Genie heard his mother. She looked in his soft brown eyes and saw fire. "So let me get my cousin!" Antonio said.

"What?" Sevenfold seemed confused. "He is not with me. This money is so my guys won't go after him, and with that happening, he is good as dead," he explained.

Antonio whipped out his pistol and let loose the whole clip—*wowp, wowp, wowp, wowp, wowp, wowp, wowp.* The monstrous shots hit two guys. The other two ran and hid. Sevenfold ran and dove behind a table. The other two started shooting from their hiding spots. They had automatic guns. Hiding behind his mother truck, Antonio looked in Genie's eyes, and she didn't look freaked out. "Let's get out of here, master," Genie yelled.

"How?" he said.

"The truck—just get in and drive off," she said.

So they did because Antonio read between the lines. The gunfire stopped long enough for them to get out of the warehouse. Genie had used her magic to jam their guns.

"What the fuck was that?" Sevenfold thought. "Why did that kid open fire like that? He took all the money except four million. He had enough to buy his life back but had no cash."

When Sleazy woke, he overheard his mother and father talking.

"I hope this teaches him a lesson: education, jail, now shot twice. This should wake him up…he's gotta see this street life is a dead end," said his father passionately.

"I agree…he's just gotta see it's a dead-end road!" added his mother. Then he shuffled a little, enough to notice if you were looking. "Thank you, Jesus. Baby, you hear me?" his mother said.

Sleazy opened his eyes. "He's awake! Oh, my baby woke up!" she yelled in joy.

Sleazy didn't feel his gunshots until his mother hugged him. He had been shot in the upper shoulder and upper arm and his left hand.

"You're coming right home when they release you, son," said his father. "This your third and final warning from God, boy. After this is death!" he yelled. "You can go back to school and get a real job," he also added.

"Yes, I also agree with your father. Your career of being a criminal is too dangerous," his mother said. "We have money. You don't have to live the way you do. This should be your wake-up call."

"Hello," said Martin.

"What's up, little brother? How you been doing? Fine seems to me!" "Sitting on all those Ms," said Sevenfold.

"Macolm, what do you want? Let me guess: you heard about Monica, right?" Martin said. "I don't owe you anything. What I did to you on Pro Street was what you needed to calm down some. "I actually helped your rep; now you seem unstoppable," he added. "Anyone else would've killed you, man; you know that."

"Well I'm not talking about that. I'm talking about those millions and that plug of yours," Sevenfold said.

"What are you talking about, millions?" Martin said.

"Your boy Antonio put up 30Ms to get his cousin from getting killed," said Sevenfold. "Thirty million!" Martin interjected. "I don't know where he got that type of money

from. I swear on my mama I don't." "Who was he with?" Martin asked.

"That fine ass girlfriend of his," Sevenfold said.

I wonder why he didn't say anything to me, Martin thought. This little motherfucker paying $30 million ransoms without telling his producer, manager. I got him a gig with Monica Roberts, and he couldn't tell me he got that type of money? I done been paying a lot of his bill, almost going broke to keep the shit up. Hell, without Monica Roberts things were starting to look bad for us.

"Get this: the little motherfucker can shoot too!" said Sevenfold. "He killed two of my security…he was packing a D-Eagle. He got some other shit going on."

"He is just a middle-class kid with talent," said Martin.

"He was pissed. He thought I tried to beat him and went nuts like he did. He did that shit before, M, I'm telling you," explained Sevenfold.

"Hold on: my first meeting with him he pulled out like 10K cash," Martin said. "Maybe he do a little hustling on the side, or something."

"I know one thing: he can definitely handle that iron," said Sevenfold. "I never heard his cousin say anything about him selling or nothing."

"As a matter of fact, he was driving a bucket when I met him," said Martin. "He just got off some lucky shots; that's all."

"Well, that shit cost me two men. I need to be paid fo' that shit, M," Sevenfold said.

"You just got 30Ms, motherfucker…same ol' Seven, huh?" Martin said in a disappointing voice.

"Naw, he drove off with twenty-seven. I got just enough to pay my connection because of his cousin's shit, and I'm flat broke," explained Sevenfold.

"Damn, don't tell me you getting extorted, Seven," Martin said. "But hold up; rewind.

This motherfucker got 27M in cash on him?"

"Yup," said Sevenfold.

"Imma call you back," said Martin then hung up.

On a PJ back to LA, Antonio was thinking hard. Damn, I done killed two people, I'm moving my mother to LA, and now I have to make more wishes to get out of all this shit, all because of Sleazy. That dude's always fucking up something, anything good. It would have Genie and his mother but under such bad terms. Then his phone started ringing. It was Martin.

"Hello," he said.

"Where are you?" said Martin.

"On my way to LAX in about thirty minutes. I got my mom and Genie with me too," said Antonio.

"OK, what about Monica?" Martin asked. "What about her?" said Antonio.

"Have y'all starting recording anything yet?" Martin asked.

"You're my manager, my fucking producer—you supposed to know all that!" Antonio quipped. "Listen, man, I have to talk to you in person," he added.

"About what?" Martin asked.

"Just be at my house in like an hour and a half, aight?" Antonio said, then hung up.

Martin knew how he was going to play this. He was going to get some of the money invested into his business. How'd that kid get that much money? Martin thought. He was going to tell him about him and the Sevenfold relationship; that would get him to trust him enough to open up. He just couldn't figure out Antonio. He was great with women, talented, and so down to earth. It seemed like magic…but that's a crazy thing, he thought.

"Listen, before you start telling me about what happened back home, I know," Martin said.

"How?" said Antonio.

"Sevenfold," Martin answered. "See, me and Sevenfold were like brothers back in the day. We sold coke, crack, and weed. We robbed banks and all. Long story short: he stole a half million from me and fucked my girl. So I shot his ass."

"Wow, really motherfucker? I could if I felt y'all had known each other," said Antonio.

Martin looked totally different in his eyes now.

"He didn't get your cousin shot either. That probably some shit he had coming. I hear he's a real dirt bag," Martin said. "But you know you can't just be running around with 27Ms in cash, right?

"I talked with Sevenfold. He's pissed you killed two of his soldiers; that also come with a price, you understand?" Martin explained.

"How much?" Antonio asked.

"A hundred K a body," Martin said.

"Aight, cool. Imma just put the rest in a safe deposit box," Antonio said.

"OK, but if you don't mind me asking, how you get that much money, man?" Martin asked. "I mean, why do all this if you could just live your life doing whatever you are doing to get that much?"

"Yeah, I don't know if I can quite trust you yet," Antonio said.

"Come on, Genie, I know this sushi place that's so good," Antonio said, leaving Martin standing on his balcony.

That's fine for right now, but Imma get some money off him either way, Martin thought as he sat on an outdoor couch on Antonio's balcony. He fired up a joint and decided that he did need to get in touch with Monica's people. *Shit*, his girl might just fuck up the whole Monica deal, Martin thought.

After a couple of weeks' healing, Sleazy needed to get out of town. Anybody could be after him now that he messed up everybody's money. He still didn't know who shot him. He was now at his mother's house, and anyone could touch him and his parents. He tried to explain to them, but they wouldn't listen. They hired guards for their house and the pool house. He needed money to get out of town, and Sevenfold's junkyard was going to be his way out. He couldn't wait. He had to hit him now while he was down. Sleazy had one girl he still could still kinda count on; it was the girl he was staying with before he was shot. He would need her to check the spot out, then be his look out. This caper would be enough to go out to California with Antonio; he had heard what he did. Sleazy didn't want to be needy also, so he still needed money for the trip. It would be perfect to be away from all the bullshit going on around town. So he called up his little shorty, and she agreed to do whatever he needed her to do. She actually wanted to do it herself because he was already hurt.

"OK, baby, that sounds good. Talk to you later, love. Bye," Sleazy said over the phone. "If it was me who had shot yo ass, you'd be dead, motherfucker," Sevenfold said.

"Oh shit, man, listen: I didn't know those guys were your people…man, I swear," Sleazy pleaded. Sevenfold had a .357 pushed against the back of Sleazy's head.

His heart had gotten him into some things. He would have to make more wishes, Genie thought. I thought he would be the one, now I will surely be back into that bottle. Years of freedom about to be a dream. He had surely gotten his family in danger. She didn't even think he liked Sleazy. He almost always spoke badly about him. I guess it's a bloodline thing that protects his own. He was going to have to think of something quick because he didn't seem to be drawing from the right source with his decision-making. Money makes people weird, and the amount he had in his position, the more they were in danger. Antonio's family and friends would test him over it. Genie didn't want to use magic but might have to. Now there is another land, starting over. At that moment Genie started to notice she was more involved than she seemed to control. Everything else relied on Antonio's next wishes.

Then it happened: someone called from an internet company wanting Antonio and his band to play a couple of songs for them. Antonio was very serious about his music. He loved it like a child, and it would get him focused on it and let him forget about everything else.

"Hello, this is Joe Gloss with Little Radio. We have an offer to make for you to play a couple songs on our platform," the voice said.

"How many followers do you have?" Antonio asked. "Two point three million," Joe said.

"OK, how much are you paying?" Antonio asked. "Seventy-five thousand dollars," Joe said.

"Cool," Antonio said. "And all I have to do is play two songs?"

"Yes, all you have to do is show up, set up, and perform any song you would like," Joe said. "We are in New York, so you would have to fly on us, of course," he explained.

"Sounds good. Just send the information to Martin Lows," Antoino said.

Damn that's almost 30K per song, he thought. He was going to give it all to his band. They would love that and know they were in the big leagues now. At that moment Antonio forgot he had just killed two people just a week ago. He then rolled up eight joints containing northern lights, moon rock, and wax and went to his studio, where he smoked and played the guitar.

Then his phone started to ring again. "Hello," he answered.

Hearing his voice changed Monica's whole intention. "Antonio, are we still doing the songs?" she blurted out.

"Hello, Monica…Yes, we are. I had so much going on at home, and I moved my mother and girlfriend out here as well," he explained.

"Oh, here I thought you were avoiding me," she said. "Well, I will call you up tomorrow to let you know when we can start recording."

"That sounds fine," Antonio said.

"Oh yeah, I gotta go to New York soon to perform for this media company called Little Radio. They're paying pretty decent," he said.

This motherfucker has a whole girl living with him and the mother now. It's starting to get weird, Monica thought.

"OK, cool. I'm kinda a busy gal Antonio!" she said.

"It just came up today. I have to talk to my manager. He's been distracted by something, but as soon as I know the date, I will fly back in that night or morning to make a song with you. You're Monica Roberts!" Antonio explained.

"OK, fine, Antonio," she said.

They haven't even recorded anything—made a song, written a song or a melody or anything. What was she thinking about? This normal guy who had a girlfriend had her sweating him. He was very normal. She hadn't even fucked him, and he had her tripping. Monica even looked him up on social media. She couldn't find him. She was so ready to meet Genie to see what she was about to make a man be faithful against her. She had to have family money and be pretty and smart to just start competing with her, Monica thought. Monica knew whatever it was, it would be great. Antonio was a very talented guitarist and would only compliment her craft. He has a soul; he could play anything she wanted on a dime. He made that guitar speak, and it was amazing. He could talk to her and make her feel normal. It's like he doesn't even see me as my achievements—just me, me, she thought. This week will be the week history is made: Monica and Antonio topping the charts with their singles doing press, media, and promotional radio. She was going to start his career off her platform with his first real songs.

"Hey, Chance, where's the wax, dude?" Monica asked her assistant. "It's in your Gucci sling bag, sis," he said.

"Oh, OK, get it for me and smear some on two joint papers and sprinkle some keef on there too," she said.

They were on their way back from her little island off the coast of China. She had been living her best life. Now it was time to come back strong. Antonio didn't know it, but he would be raised up straight into stardom instantly. His girlfriend probably couldn't handle it.

Martin's phone rang.

"Hello," he answered.

"Man, what the fuck been going on with you? You about to fuck up a million-dollar deal. Monica's calling me, talking 'bout when we gonna do some music. I got a gig all the way in New York for 75K. Motherfucker, this your job!" Antonio yelled.

"You already a millionaire, motherfucker. Why it matters?" a coked-up Martin said. "Man, what's going on with you? First you give me the crazy news Sevenfold's your dog; now you fucking up million-dollar deals," he said.

"Fuck that, dude. You got 30Ms to give away for a grease-ball cousin who don't care about you nor his mother or father," Martin said. "I gave you two million and a car, and you out here moving with that kinda money. I believe in you, man. I move us out here and put you around the biggest stars on the planet, and you do me like that, dude."

"You knew you was going to make money off me anyways, dude. That's why you did it. Now we about to make music with the best out here, man…Fuck that. Just be makin' that happen with Monica, and we good," Antonio said.

"Aight, dude, but you know it's bullshit," Martin said.

Why the hell am I fucking this up? This is major for me too, he thought. I'm back on my shit from today on; who cares if he got money? Some people do; some people don't. There are a lot of opportunities in this deal as well. I get the young man frustration; I'd be mad too.

Sevenfold—it's him with his way of being negative in everything.

"Now that I got your attention, like, make some money now. Sit yo ass down," Sevenfold said as he cocked the hammer back.

"I know you didn't know about those Africans. Nobody did; that was a favor for some crazy motherfuckers. I had to pay them millions for those fools you shot up. Thankfully your cousin got bank or all of us would be dead—me, you, him, his family, my family. They got the firepower," Sevenfold explained. "I'm here to let you know we are going to get rich off your cousin, and you lucky I'm even paying you. I bet if I told him you got his brother killed for 50K, he'd kill you himself, huh?" Sevenfold said with a grin.

"Man, you ain't gotta do all that. You know I'm down for whatever when it comes to making this loot," Sleazy said. "Cuz punk ass ain't gonna do shit. That motherfucker not soft, but he ain't no killer."

"Bullshit. He killed B. J. and Tone like it was nothing," Sevenfold interjected. "Nah, not Tonio," said Sleazy.

"Bo, you think Imma make that up?" Sevenfold said. "I saw it: that fool like a marksman."

Damn where the fuck—who the fuck is Antonio now? Sleazy thought. He running around with big Ms murkin people…Damn. Fucking a bad, bad bitch riding with him. It's gotta be something with that bitch. She just came from nowhere; no one know her or anything. Imma find out about her too, he thought.

"Whatever it takes to get it, it gotta be gotten," Sleazy said.

This little motherfucker is poison from hell, Sevenfold thought. He thought he would have to kill him now, but fuck it—I can just use him for now, he thought. Sitting here shot up from whatever, and planning to escort his own cousin, who just put up 30Ms for his life. Come to think about it, he kinda reminds me of me when I was younger, he thought.